I0548176

Table Of Contents

I wanted to thank everyone for helping me and supporting me while I wrote my first book.
I would like to thank my wife for sticking by me for the long 3 year process. I would like to thank all my friends in my life for also supporting me and keeping me focused on finishing the book. I am very grateful and I appreciate all of you!

https://www.facebook.com/pages/Shuttered-past

SHUTTERED PAST

WRITTEN BY DEREK SCHUG

CHAPTER ONE

It started one morning; I couldn't remember anything, I didn't know what happened, it was like something entered my body and took my memory. I could only remember my name and where I lived.

My name is John Storm; I live in Howard lake Minnesota. I'm 25 years old and am a college student at the U of M. I need to figure out what happened to my memory and why it happened. What part in my past brought this on? These questions I have will be answered if I have to spend all night doing it. A knock on my door startled me, but when I went to answer it, the phone rang so I answered it quick. "Hello?" I said frustrated with the situation. What happened next really freaked me out. "Remember!" Then they hung up. I approached the door and opened it, and there stood my friend Drew Feltzers, a college buddy and a childhood friend. We grew up on the same block with my other best friend Sammy Dells; we used to play football every day from sun up to sun down. A whole lot of memories we had. Then I wondered why can I remember my friends but not my life with family or love life? "What's up Sammy?" I asked. "Man we got to get to class, its 11am what are you doing in your boxers" He asked hysterically. "Man shit is just crazy today, I don't think I'll make it to class, just have a lot going on." I said pacing the floor, I was getting dizzy from pacing I decided to sit down and grabbed water. Sammy just stared at me for a while thinking hard on the words he should say. "Dude, so there was this chick last night right? Man she was nice, you should have seen her" He said trying to cheer me up.

I laughed it off and told him I would catch up with him later. I wondered what I did last night but nothing came to mind it was a blank. I just couldn't understand what the hell happened. Now that I was getting mad and frustrated I decided I would hit the gym for a few hours, blow off some steam. I get to the gym and it says they're closed for repairs. "How could they be closed?" I thought out loud. I figured since it was nice outside I would go for a 5 mile jog and clear my head, but as soon as I went to jog a cop approached me. "Son, I'm going to have to take you down to the station for questioning." He said in a stern voice. "Can I ask why?" I said with a confused look on my face. "Sir, just come with me I'll explain at the station." So I got into the cop car and as we get to the station and I see a woman, crying in the chair at the desk. I walk over to her and ask "are you ok ma'am?" I asked with a look of concern on my face. She looked up at me for a few moments and then gave me a hug, stunned by this I stood there and then slowly put my arms around her.

"I'm glad you're ok son" she cried. If the day couldn't get any weirder I looked at her and said "ma'am, I'm sorry but I don't know who you are, but thanks for your concern I guess." The cop pulled me aside and told me that the woman says she's my mother, but I didn't know who she was. So I went along with it and asked the lady "what happened that she was in so much hurt." All of a sudden everything got dark and cold as if a blackout has happened. But in that split second of darkness it seems as if it lasted a life time. I was going to repeat my question to the lady but she was gone. Freaked out by the situation I headed back home. The walk home seemed eerie as well, like I was being watched but I ignored it and just stayed on my path. I finally got to my dorm, exhausted from the events that day I thought I would take a nap for a few hours and I will figure everything out later. As I was laying there trying to sleep, thoughts rushed through my head. Who was this lady? Why did she claim to be my mother? I finally dozed off and I had a dream, but it wasn't a normal dream it was dark and cold, like when I was at the police station. What does it mean? The dream went on and I saw that lady again and she kept repeating something but I couldn't hear her. "What are you saying?" I screamed, but I couldn't even hear myself. She kept getting closer, repeating the same thing but I still couldn't hear her. Then as she got close to me she vanished. I then woke up in a cold sweat, I couldn't catch my breath, and I gathered myself back to reality and told myself it was just a dream. A knock on the door louden the silence of the room, "who is it?" I asked. "It's me Drew! Open up." I went to answer the door and he seemed out of place with himself. As if he wasn't himself. So I slapped him in the face as a joke to see if he would snap out of his trans. "Dude, what the hell was that for?" "You seemed like you were in outer space, sorry for that." I said as I laughed it off. "Well it wasn't funny! John." He yelled. "What's going on with you john?" he asked in a concerning tone. "Nothing bro just a lot on my mind, I Just have to figure shit out." I said. I asked him to leave and I was just not feeling myself. I don't know how to deal with the events that have happened. So I decided to make a doctor's appointment and see if there is anything they can find.

A few days went by and I was still waiting to get into the doctor but still no call. "I think I'm going to go for a walk" I thought out loud. With weird dreams, and not being able to sleep because of them I've been doing a lot of walking. I sat down about 4 blocks away from the college on a bench. I felt I was being watched again, so I looked around and I couldn't see anyone I didn't see on a normal basis. All of a sudden I wasn't on the bench anymore. I must have blacked out again. This time it was worse than last time. I felt weak, I couldn't think, I felt lost and felt sick. "Hello!!!!" I screamed. "Is anyone there?" It was dark and cold, which has been the pattern. Again I saw someone, but this time it was an old man, tall with grey hair. He was walking funny and mumbling some words, I tried to read his lips but he was speaking to fast I couldn't make out what he was saying. Then he started running toward me like a crazy person, so I started to run away but it feels as if I wasn't going anywhere. At this point I was getting really scared and with tears running down my face I yelled "Leave me alone! Why are you chasing me? Who are you?" I kept screaming. I eventually fell to the ground and I looked behind me and he is nowhere to be seen. When I finally woke up, I was the hospital. The doctor told me I was screaming and causing a scare for the people walking outside. He asked me if I had any illnesses, I told him I didn't know. "Why were you lying on that bench screaming?" he asked "I'm not sure, I remember sitting on the bench and then I woke up here." I said. Then doctor gave me some water and something to calm my nerves. "Well, son you're lucky to be alive, so go home get some rest and try to sleep in your own bed for now on." He said as he chuckled and walked away.

CHAPTER TWO

As I get back to my dorm I found a note addressed to me. I looked over the envelope but I didn't see a name on it anywhere. I set it down on my desk and sat on my bed, still trying to get over what happened between the time I sat on the bench and till I woke up in the hospital. I concluded that every time I have a blackout or a dream I wake up somewhere else or in a daze. "What does it mean?" I thought aloud. I thought about reading the note I found a few times, not knowing what it was or what was in it. It was nerve racking considering everything I've been through, so I opened it anyway.

"I know who you are; I know what you are looking for. I know everything about you and what you want to know, I'm the one who killed your loved ones, family, friends, girlfriend. I'm everywhere; I can see you day and night. When you're sleeping and when you were at the police station the other day. If I were you I would stop while you're behind John. I am what you fear, what lurks in the shadows. Don't come looking for me, because you will be seeing me soon, very soon. Have a nice day sweet heart."

I could only stare blankly at the writing on the letter. My hands were trembling, thoughts racing, fear growing, My emotions were out of control, and all I could think about were who it could be, the old man in my dreams or the lady at the police station? There are so many questions and no answers. As tears roll down my face all I could wonder is who was this girlfriend the person in the note was talking about. I was getting tired but I tried to stay awake due to the bad dreams I've been having lately. I lay my head gently onto my pillow thinking of happy thoughts, but I'm getting these flash backs that I don't remember knowing were still in my memory. I see a young woman early 20's, and a man around the same age, holding a baby. I couldn't see who they were holding but they were happy, then the dream skipped ahead, a person in school with a blurred out face and a very pretty girl talking to him.

She was blonde, body tight, busty, apple bottom. I still couldn't understand why I can't ever hear anyone talking in my dreams, maybe I'm not supposed to, maybe I'm just supposed to remember. I was awoken to the phone ringing; in between awake and asleep I answered it. A man on the other end called me by name and said I was to attend the 5yr high school reunion, so I agreed and hung up the phone. I don't know why I didn't think of this before, but I could look at my yearbooks for clues. If I have a high school reunion I have to have yearbooks. As I was frantically looking for these books a knock at the door stopped me in my tracks. A crack of thunder made me jump, so now I'm assuming different scenarios before I answered the door. "Who is it?" I asked hesitantly as I walked toward the door. They pounded on the door and startled me, and again I asked who it was. So I told myself to suck it up and open it, "boo!!" what are you doing goof ball?" a girl from school shouted as I looked out the door. "You scared me Jenna!" I shouted and trying to get my heart rate back to normal. As she leaned in to kiss me on the cheek I backed up a little confused with her intentions. "You don't want me to kiss you john? We only are dating goof." She said looking depressed. "We're dating? I don't remember how is it possible? If you're my girlfriend you should be dead? I stuttered. "What do you mean dead? We've been dating 2 years john, if you don't want to be together any more I'll leave and never come back." She cried as she headed toward the door. "No, wait! I have to talk to you about something." I said as I hurried over to her before she opened the door. I asked her to sit on the bed and I explained to her everything that has been going on the past few weeks. She was in tears as I was telling her this; I told her I had no other way to say it.

Before Jenna left for the night I asked her to be my date for the high school reunion. She graciously said yes, and the next day we headed to the school. We mingled and had a great time, talked to old friends and heard that one of our teachers had past. Saw old friends, and ex-friends who tormented me all through school. The whole night I was thinking of different ways to ask Jenna about who my family was. But I thought a full night of fun would be great for everyone before we get into something that could end up being dangerous, but I need to know everything.

And right before the night was to end, everything went dark again. All I could think of was not now; I just want to move on from this today. This time no one showed up, it was silent for a moment. Then all I hear are words "I told you to stop while you were behind john, I'll see you soon"

When I came to, I was back in my bed alone. The next day after lunch I had invited Jenna, Sammy, and drew over to go over the events that have been going on with me. After about 2 hours of explaining and re-explaining for Drew's sake, everyone knows he's a little slow in the head after we had a falling out in the 7th grade. Sammy went first and started back a few years, he told me that there was an accident, and stated that a few people died and there were a ton of injuries. Then Jenna and Sammy chimed in and said that I was in a coma for 4yrs. But then I thought to myself, "How did I graduate high school and make it to college?" Drew continued, before you awoke from the coma, your father…your father had a heart attack. Your mother moved away and they had enough money put away to keep the hospital bills paid. "I'm sorry john, we wanted to tell you but we just didn't know how to." He said choking up. "Do you know how the accident happen guys? " I asked urgently, they told me they weren't sure how it happened, but the news that day reported a dark mass in the road and that the police said it wasn't anything to worry about. Sammy didn't really have anything to say but Jenna told me everything I needed to know. She told me that my parents loved me very much and not to worry about them. She then told me something that just scared me shitless, my father left me something before he died, but I don't know what it would be. She told me that it was important and that I would need it someday. "Was it like a box of never expiring condoms or something?" I joked. We all had a little laugh and decided to call it a night, Sammy and drew left and Jenna stayed the night to make sure I was going to be alright. The next afternoon I looked up the accident that happened with me and my parents. I looked in horror, all those people, cars on fire, even an explosion accrued 4 cars behind my parent's car. The reporter said that a teenage boy was rescued but the father had died and the mother was in critical condition. I couldn't watch any longer and turned it off.

CHAPTER THREE

I was distraught the whole night. Pacing the floor and had a nervous feeling like something bad was going to happen. All of a sudden I felt like my equilibrium was off.

So I sat down and standing in my door was a young woman, she just stared at me like she was contemplating something. But something seemed familiar her mouth was moving like the others, just couldn't hear the words. The same thing happened with the other 2 people I saw. I asked her, "what do you want from me?" just then it got dark and cold, like before but this time I didn't feel in danger. It felt more like a vision, or a flashback, I saw Sammy, and Jenna along with drew. They were talking in a hospital but I didn't see who they were looking over. I got a little bit closer and it was me, lying there, unresponsive. I overheard them talking and I didn't know if I should believe it or not. They seemed to be very upset with Sammy like he caused my accident. He stated he didn't know what had happened and they agreed that they wouldn't speak of it again. Drew had asked Sammy what had happened to him that he doesn't remember.

Sammy just looked blankly into space, then just uttered some words but for some reason I couldn't hear it anymore. So it must be something I'm not supposed to know, or it's something I have to figure out for myself. But it's getting old and I'm not very patient. When I finally snapped out of the Trans I was in, the woman was gone. There was still more I had to find out, so I decided I was going to go find my mother, in hopes to rid this memory loss. I spent a few days looking up her name I got from Jenna, and it seems she doesn't want to be found. But I'm not going to stop till I do. Then after a few more days I finally found her, but there was a problem, it seemed she died a few months ago the reasons were unknown. I thought to myself how it could be unknown. After the flash back of my friends in the hospital with me, I decided I can't trust anyone, I'll have to do this on my own. I called the cemetery where my mother was buried, or was supposed to be buried. The girl on the other end told me there was no record of her being there and that a body fitting her description was removed a few days after the burial service. When I got off the phone, I was just in shock of what I have found out. Why would a body be removed after a few days? Is there something bigger than me going on? And what am I going to find out?

All these questions and no answers again frustrate me. I called all my friends to come over so I can tell them I was taking a leave of school and that I don't know when I'd be back. They looked at me with concern and in a state of shock. "I will miss you all, and I will be back." I told them without choking up. So I'm headed back to Howard Lake, MN if I'm going to find answers it will have to be there. I drove what seemed to be hours, blasting my favorite country station. Sun was shining nice cool breeze and for 2 days I haven't had a dark out or strange person trying to terrorize me. As I was getting into my home town, I started getting blurry vision and thinking to myself "could it be starting up again?" I rubbed my eyes and kept rolling. I stopped at a nearby bar to figure out what's going on. All of a sudden the reoccurring darkness appeared it's not that I'm even fearful of this anymore but more annoyed and ready to rid this. This time all 3 people are there staring at me, the man, the old lady, and the young woman.

Who are they and what do they want from me? I stood there looking at all 3 of them waiting for a reaction of some kind. "What do you want from me? I asked getting frustrated I ran up to them but I couldn't move, like something was holding me back. "Answer me! What have I done to deserve this?" they looked at each other and at once they said "soon you will know the truth, soon." As they vanished an even darker presence arrived not in physical form but an eerie voice that said "I told you to stop, john. This is your last warning." Then I woke up and it was 9pm I've been out for 7hrs. I figured I'm not safe anymore and I need to figure this out fast, what if I'm driving and I have a dark out, so many lives could be at risk including my own. What truth were the three flashers talking about? I headed over to the library to do some research on the flash backs and visions I've been having, maybe it happen to someone else or if I'm really just going crazy. I was searching and searching and I came up with people that were mysteriously forgetting certain events and a few cases where people just one day forgot everything. A couple hours go by and I find this video of a kid who is going through what I am now, he states that it went on for months, and he never could find a way to get rid of the flashers. In some cases he said he was physically harmed after waking up from being attacked while unconscious. And so far I have no bodily harm…yet. He goes on to say that he found a way to suppress the dark outs. But never went into detail which doesn't help me much. I watched his last video posted and it was terrifying, he was in total fear and after 5 minutes into the video he screams and blood splatters all over the screen and a dark face appears and it goes dark. His computer must have an auto-submit to post on the site, because there is no way he could have. After seeing this, I was even more scared for what is to come. So what does that mean for me? I must stop this from happening to me and everyone else. When I go to leave Jenna appears out by my car, "what are you doing here? I didn't even tell you where I was going." I explained. "You're so predictable, john. We have been watching you." She said with a creepy look at her face. "Excuse me? Watching me? Are you guys insane?" I yelled. "Yes, to make sure you are doing ok, john we're worried about you." She frantically told me. As I said I can't trust anyone.

Her movements, her speech all seemed weird. No one watches someone, so I put this in the back of my mind. "How is everyone back at school?" I asked. She had told me that they guys have disappeared and she doesn't know where they went, and that my dorm was destroyed like someone was looking for something important. "What is so important in my dorm room? I don't have anything of importance in there, except for…never mind I need to go" I urgently told her. "Except for what!" she yelled as I was driving away. I went to look in my rear view mirror and she was gone. Either my mind is playing tricks on me or she is really fast.

I stopped by my old house that my parents still owned even after their passing, I looked through old photos, and something strange was going on, every picture had this pattern in the background. Like something was always surrounding my family. I found my parents old HD video camera, so I decided since nothing could get any worse I would make a good bye video.

"Hi, I'm John if you're seeing this something bad has happened. For the past month I've been dealing with some things, dark things that I can't even explain without looking crazy. Both my parents were killed long ago, by a force which I would like to believe are the flashers. They can take you into your mind and either trap you or trick you into believing what they want you to, unless you can get out first. I have experienced this first hand. I know; I know I sound crazy but this is really happening. My friends are acting weird and I have no one to go back on or too. I've been losing sleep nothing seems real anymore, I just want it to end. So I leave you with this, I love you all and one day we will meet again and no one will get hurt anymore."

When I turned the camera off, I placed the disc into a folder and left it on the table. I heard some rumbling outside and it sounds like a storm is coming. "I will just stay in tonight, and try to relax" I thought to myself. So I turned on the fire place, and relax on the couch. I was going over all of the events that have happened so far. 1. Old lady in the police station. 2. The old guy and what was he mumbling. 3. The young woman in my dorm, why did she show me that event in the hospital? 4. My friends watching me and Jenna disappearing. I'm hoping to get all these answered but it's getting late and I need some much needed rest.

I was worried about not getting any sleep so I popped some sleeping tablets and drifted off. My dream was going good so far, just as normal a dream as any. My parents were there, friends weren't so creepy around me. Everyone was happy. Then this object kept appearing around in the dream. What was it? It looked familiar. When I woke up the next morning I felt refreshed. I walked outside to find a package was left for me. It's curious because I never ordered anything. And no one knows I'm here.

I felt hesitant to open it, but what could be worse than what I've been through.

CHAPTER FOUR

In the package I found a note, an old camera, and a blank picture.

"Welcome home, son. We've been waiting for you. In this box you will find an old camera. Be careful with it. It's very valuable and can help you if you figure out how to use it. Use it wisely if it lands in the wrong hands the world is in danger. Next is the blank picture. This is not a good picture, this is your future. Nothing is left. I've said too much and must go now."

Who sent this to me? I didn't see a postage tag. I don't see how this old camera can help me, it's old. And the blank picture is the frightening one; I can't believe that's my future. Does that mean I fail at finding a way out of this, or is it the current path I'm on? "I think I'm going to need help with this after all" I said to myself. I called my friends and they told me they would make it out as soon as they could, which I would hope was soon. All I could do is pace around looking at the stuff I got in the box, wondering how to use it other than its original purpose. Next I hear the phone ringing, "hello?" I don't hear anyone on the other end... so I asked again. Then all I hear is breathing, and screaming. "John run, Get out go!" my eyes widen when I hear this. "Don't take them! No, please." Who is the other voice on the phone? It kind of sounds like me, But I haven't seen them. Is this a trick? Then I hear a dark groan and the line goes dead. Could this be a call from a future event? Why can't I figure this crap out? I'm getting tired of having questions.

A few hours later my friends finally showed up. "What took you guys so long to get here?" I asked. "We had some things to take care of first." Sammy said. For the past few days I've noticed my friends have been acting weird. And all I could think about was the vision I had in the hospital, and them talking around me. Could it be true? I don't want to confront them about it just yet. "Let's search this house for any clues or anything of use" I yelled. So we scattered around looking for something. I didn't plan on living here once we finished so leaving a mess was none of my concern. So far I have a camera and a blank photo, weird objects to have to help your memory. I went to look in the one of the bedrooms and I heard a big crash sound coming from up in the attic, "what is going on" I thought. I told them to look for something not break anything. So I went to check it out, and when I got up there I didn't see anyone, just darkness. "Is anyone up here" I asked. I got nothing in response. So I turned my flash light on, and I saw a black figure moving about up here. My knees were shaking and I could see my breath, but it was 73 in the house, so how could I see my breath?

I wondered. As I was walking around I found a box of my dad's old stuff. There were medals, awards, and a do not open box. I put the box aside as for it could be useful later. "I'm coming for you" someone whispered in my ear. I was sweating and I couldn't breathe and I was shaking. All I could think was "what was that? And why won't it show itself to me." Then I see a black mass coming at me from the shadows, it was moving really fast, and I can't move. But what happened next was more shocking. That woman I saw in my dorm showed up and blasted the dark mass away from me, right before it could hit me. I was then able to move and could talk and breathe. "Thank-you" I said. But she was gone. "What is going on?" I yelled. My friends raced up to check on me, "John you ok?" they yelled. "Yea, I'm fine; this black mass attacked me and I couldn't move and a woman I've seen before protected me and stopped it from hurting me." I explained. "Do you know who it could be? Drew asked quietly. "No bro I don't, but I have my theories, also I found this box, I don't know what it means. But it has the words "do not open" on it." I told them.

"Let's open it up and see what is in it" Sammy yelled out as he laughed. We took a vote and decided we weren't going to open it just yet. Sammy was pretty bummed but there is a time a place for things. I really wanted to talk to Jenna, and see how she was doing. "Hey Jenna, do you think we could find a place to be alone for a while" I asked softly. We told the guys we would be right back and just to keep looking. And I could her Sammy softly laugh and say "they're so going to do it" I just laugh it off and we head up to the upstairs to my old bedroom. We talked for about an hour or so, got things off our chest, put everything out there. I told her thank you for the talk and I put a soft kiss on her cheek. As I was going to get up she had lifted her shirt off and walked towards me and we started to passionately kiss and hold each other close. I gently laid her down on the bed and kissed her body softly watching her mouth as she was reaching a sexual high. She then proceeded to climb on top of me and as we stared into each other's eyes, we seemed to be lost in the moment of heavy breathing and euphoria. I finally asked her about why they all were acting so weird and I told her about the vision I had. She looked like she was upset about it, and looked at me like I just killed her cat. "How do you know about the hospital" she asked. I told her that a strange woman came into my dream and showed it to me. And I told her I didn't know if I believed it or not. She assured me it was a trick and not to believe it.

Jenna got up from the bed and finished getting dressed. I watched as she walked out like she was worried about something. "Jenna! What's wrong?" I yelled out as the door calmly shuts. I sat there wondering, and thinking what just happened. I want to believe that there is nothing wrong with my friends. I walked down stairs see them talking amongst themselves, they looked at me like I did something wrong. "Hey guys, I think I'm going to get out of here for a while and clear my head. "Why, we still have things to go through to help you bud" Sammy expressed.

I told him that they could finish up and I wouldn't be long. As I was walking around town, I stopped at the grocery store as I was feeling kind of hungry. I looked around for about an hour and nothing really caught my eye. So I left to go meet back up with the guys, and just then cop cars and a fire truck came speeding past and startled me. "What the hell is going on" I asked myself. So I ran after them and come to find out my house is burning to the ground. "NO!!!!!!!" I screamed with tears rolling down my face. I tried to run to my front door to see if my friends got out and 3 police officers stopped me in my tracks. "My friends, my... I have to get to them" I told the police officer. "Son, no one was found, fire fighters searched the whole area, and there was nothing left in the house after the explosion. As I dropped to my knees in shock all I could think about were my friends. How could this happen in 2 hours. I didn't even hear an explosion. As the cops were leaving, it all seemed like slow motion. A half hour goes by and I'm still on my knees in front of the rubble that used to be my house. Then it hit me, all the stuff that was in that box is gone. As I was getting ready to get up and leave, a small glow caught my eye. In the rubble was a glowing box, could it be the stuff left for me? As I opened the box a giant flash exploded in my eyes and I woke up back in my house, I screamed for everyone and they rushed into the room and looked startled. "What's wrong bro?" drew shouted. "You... you guys are dead, an explosion" I wiped my cheeks as they were wet from crying. "It was all a dream, how is this possible? It all seemed so real.

"Ok, guys I think we need to go somewhere else and set up some kind of base that is far from here. This place isn't safe for us to be. "Where are we going to go?" they all said. I didn't really know but somewhere that I could keep an eye on everyone.

CHAPTER 5

It's been 3 weeks since we left Howard Lake; it feels like my blackouts are increasing, it's a never ending headache. I stood outside, looking at the sun set. It was Bright orange with a little red, with a slight breeze blowing through my hair. It was an unsettling silence. "Hey john, what are you doing out here so early?" drew said groggy from just waking up. "Just thinking man, I just need to figure things out." I said optimistically. Drew and I walked back into our new home in green city, it seemed like a quite place and we didn't know anyone. "Hey guys, who did you, sleep last night? I made breakfast" Jenna said as she laughed. We all said yes, and dug into eggs and bacon. We were all having a good time, and then I could feel the blackout coming on. Then it hit me out of no where. "Hello?" I called out as my voice echoed. "Anyone there?" nothing but silence, it doesn't seem like the other blackouts.

"I've been waiting for you John, I warned you for the last time. Stop what you're doing, you will not stop us." I was frozen in fear, I felt alone. "Why haven't woken up from this yet?" I thought to myself. I walked for what seemed like for ever, no end in sight. As I was walking all I could hear is yelling and my name being called, then I woke up gasping for air. My friends were sitting around me and staring at me like I just came back to life. There eyes were wide and they looked worried. "John, you scared the shit out of us. What happened?" "I don't know guys, one second I'm talking to you guys then the next I blacked out." I explained, and not telling them that I can feel when it will happen. "How long was I out this time?" they looked at each other for a moment, then looked back at me..."13 hours john." drew said with a concerned tone.

I could only stare in shock, not moving a muscle and not even to blink. How could I be out for 13 hours? I thought to myself. I finally got to my feet still in shock from the news; I bolted out the front door without saying a single goodbye. I don't know where I'm going, all I know is I need to go somewhere. my friends have something to do with what's going on with me I'm just sure of it, but right now I cant prove it. I stopped at a local park, and at least there is a bunch of people around to call for help in case of another blackout. I sat at a bench just watching parents play with their kids having fun and laughing, and just thinking of my parents and how I could have lost them so early in life. I need to find my mom, figure when to open that box, and find out what the camera and blank photo is for.

But right now finding out where my mom is my top priority. I went back to the house and everyone was sleeping so I grabbed some things and box. I thought about leaving a note but I can't be stopped, it's along road ahead and I feel my friends are holding me back from this puzzle. It was about a quarter after three in the afternoon. I was going to take a bus to scene of the accident to try and find some clues. Without looking back I boarded the last bus out of town, I should be in Oklahoma City soon enough. It was about an hour or two into the trip and as I stared around at the people on the bus, I didn't know anyone nor even have I seen them before. It could just be me being paranoid, I took a couple aspirin to help with my recent headache, and I tried to document the travel by noticing trees, buildings and street signs. I don't know why I was doing this or what made me think of it but it seems as if it would help me know where I am. The aspirin I took must have caused me to fall asleep, because when I woke up I wasn't on the bus, I was in an emergency room. I looked around and I had a ringing in my ears and things were blurry, I kept screaming for help and a nurse with a low cut red shirt and a V-cut lab coat came over to me.

"Are you ok, can you hear me?" she asked but it was muffled, I explained I couldn't hear her very well, she checked me over for about 5 minutes and I could hear clearly again. "My name is cherish, and I will be your nurse" she said to me, while people were crying and screaming around me. "What happened?" I asked frantically. "Sir, you were in a car accident" she said to me with a confused look on her face. "Did you not know you were in an accident? She asked, "No, no I didn't, I must have fell asleep" I shouted. I looked toward the floor trying to think about what could have happened to cause an accident, I saw a TV in the corner of the room with the news on with footage of the accident. "I'm Donna Jones with shinning news, and I'm here at the scene of a horrifying accident. 23 people killed, and over 59 people injured." She explained, I then tried to drown out the sound and I kept watching and I saw the paramedics putting what seemed to be lifeless body on a stretcher. "oh my god" I thought to myself, my friends will see me and try to find me, so I tried to get out of there as fast as possible. But I was stopped by 2 doctors and 2 policemen. "Son, I can't allow you to leave yet, we have to make sure you don't have a concussion. And these gentlemen would like to have a word with you." what would they want to talk to me for, it's not like I caused the accident or anything.

"Son my name is officer Jonathan and this is officer Scotts, do you remember anything from the bus that could help us?" they asked suspiciously asked. I didn't answer them because I really didn't have an answer to give. "Son, if you anything you need to tell us. We have footage of the bus accident." they explained. I shot my head up, and asked if I could watch the footage of the crash. For 30min I watched in horror as the bus was being torn apart and bodies flying, we couldn't see who or what was doing it, but after another hour of watching in silence all 3 of us jumped out of our seats in shock. We stayed silent for a little while longer and one of the officers turned to me and said "son...umm, you have the right to remain silent, anything you do or say can be used against you in the court of law. You have the right to an attorney, if you don't have one, one will be appointed to you.

I stayed silent unable to move, until one of the officers tried to put the handcuffs on me. I was using moves I didn't know I could, I grabbed the officers arm and twisted it to almost the breaking point, and the other officer tried to stop me and I handcuffed both of them to the steel table in the room and threw there guns to the other corner of the room. "I'm sorry officers, but it couldn't have been me, please, please forgive me." I cried. I walked out of the office calmly like nothing happened, I grabbed my things and I left. I walked for about 3 miles before I called a cab, to go from one accident scene to one that happened many years ago. It seemed very overwhelming but I have to get through it.

Chapter 6

Here I am, 4 days have passed since the accident and I was in Oklahoma. There was an eerie presence ever since I got into state; I stopped at a local market for food and water I was running low on supplies as well. I had lost most of it on the bus and I really need some aspirin. My headaches have increased in the last couple days. As I was walking around the Town of Oak River, people seemed to be whispering and staring at me like they knew me. I stopped a gentleman and asked if he knew me, he just looked at me for a moment then, had a look on his face of fear like he just saw a ghost. He just walked away with the scared look on his face; I spent most of the day wondering why the people here are afraid of me. I decided that today was the day I would open the box I wasn't supposed to open, but I'm sick of waiting and it's like its calling out to me. As I was going to open the box my phone rang, it startled me "hello?" I said slowly, "john, where the hell have you been the passed month? We are all worried about you. We saw you on the news." drew yelled. "I'm fine, and please don't worry I just have things I need to figure out on my own for now, and I'm ok." I calmly told him. "Well while you were on you're little adventure, and leaving us in the dark, Jenna left as well. We don't know where she went." Sammy interrupted. "Guys I..." I froze as I was going to defend myself, but I saw what looked to be like my mom. I hung up on the guys and followed her, but when I finally caught up to her it was just a random local. I apologized to the lady and headed toward a hotel to stay the night.

The next morning I couldn't wake up, it was like I was in a paralyzed state. I was getting really annoyed with these random blackouts and now I can't wake up. In what I think is a dream I had visions of the box, and the camera and photo. What does it all mean? I thought to myself, I saw Jenna and the guys again but this time we weren't in the hospital like before.

We were at a cemetery, it was raining, everyone covered in black and crying. But I couldn't see the grave stones. Only the faces of the people and that's it. And then it all disappeared and I woke up to paramedics reviving me. Before they had a chance to ask questions I got out of there, I wasn't going to jail for the incident at the hospital. I tried to find a quite place to think and open this damn box but I couldn't find anywhere safe to do so. I was walking down by a strip mall and I noticed this white envelope lying on the ground, wondering why no one has picked it up, I reached down and grabbed it. I went into the coffee shop nearby and thought I would take a rest. I stared at it for awhile debating if I should open it, not knowing if it was someone's mail or not. So I took a risk and tore it open, and it read

"John, we have been watching you. This will be the one and last warning

Stop searching for your past, ever since you were young you have been stubborn and a fighter but it stops here.

You will not be warned again. We will have what we came for and you brat like you will not stand in our way."

I quickly got up and threw it away so no one else can see it, and maybe I should just give up and go back home. Nothing seems to be getting easier here.

I stayed at the hotel for one more day and I'm going to catch the next bus out of here in the morning. In the back of my mind it feels like something bad is going to happen, I couldn't quite figure out what it was though. I was just about to fall asleep when a pounding at the door startled me. "Why does this keep happening to me, can I never just sleep, damn." "Hurry up open the door; please." a voice said on the other side of the door. As I opened the door a kid pushed it open and it was so hard I fell to the floor. "What the fuck was that for kid?" I yelled. "Sorry, I really didn't mean it. Are you him, are you the guy?" he said pacing the floor. "I am a guy yes, but what guy are you talking about?" I said confused.

He told me that he saw my video on Youtube and that he too is having the same blackouts and visions I have. I thought he was messing with me at first, but his story was pretty accurate to mine. He had a suit case with him, and when I asked him about it he told me it was a secret. After a few hours of talking and him pacing he finally opened the suit case and I was pretty shocked to see what was in there. He had years of logs and videos he kept. He told me he only had a few days left to live. When I asked him why he didn't say a word, in fact he didn't move for 6hrs. I almost called an ambulance, until I realized that it reminds me of my own blackouts. "What happened to me?" he said in a daze. "You blacked out; it happens to me a lot sometimes everyday." I explained. He told me that he is giving me his logs and videos to look through and see if I can find an explanation of what is going on with me. A few hours later he died. Before I called the police, I examined him to see how he died. His eyes were black and his skin was pail white like he was scared of something before he died.

CHAPTER 7

So I'm on my way back to Howard lake, I let the guys know I was coming back. The last few weeks have been interesting, get into a bus accident, beat up a couple of cops and watched a kid die in front of my eyes. Why does this happened to me I wonder, I don't do drugs and I rarely drink. I keep thinking back to the first day it happened and none of it makes sense. I would be so pissed if this was a dream and someone was reading my story in the paper and none of this was real. If it was a dream I would have woke up by now, and speaking of being awake I need to get some sleep. Haven't slept well with everything going to hell and all, all I could think about was Jenna. "Where has she gone?" I wondered. As I sat on the bus ride home a kid got on the last stop, he was short and had a little facial hair, with a hat on backwards and came over and sat next to me. "What the fuck is up man?" he shouted. I looked at him for a moment. "You look familiar do I know you?" I asked softly. He stated he was my brother, our mother remarried. "My name is Jason, but most people call me mike. Don't ask I don't know why they do that. You're john right? I've heard so much about you, mom talked about you all the time." he exclaimed. "Where have you been all my life?" I cried as we hugged it out. "Moms been sick and she told me to never find you, but didn't give me a reason, she left years ago and I haven't been able to find her." he told me. I had a feeling he was holding more back then what he was telling me, but I didn't care because I got to me my brother. "So are you going to hang around with me for while?" I asked anxiously. "I don't know I have money to make and girls to flirt with" he laughed. I finally got him to come join me on my journey; it will be nice to have someone I can talk to besides my friends who I can't trust right now. But you can always trust family.

When we finally got back to Howard Lake, my brother told me he was going to going to go to bed since we talked the whole way up here. I felt better that I had him around, I walked into the kitchen of the hotel we were staying in. and I set the box down on the table. I could stare at this thing all day, but every time I go to open it I get interrupted or something bad happens. I've thought about destroying it, but that wouldn't do me any good if I really need it to save my friends, my family and myself. "Fuck it" I said out loud, I opened the box really fast, a really bright light flashed in front of my eyes. "You, you again?" I said under my breath. "Yes, I came to stop you from what you're about to do, if you go forward with this, you and your friends will die." she shouted. "I don't care anymore, my friends need me. I am sick of waiting!" I shouted. She then nodded her head and disappeared. I looked in the box, I found besides my camera, the blank photo, I found sunglasses, a small mirror, a big pocket knife and harmonica. "What am I going to do with all of these?" I thought to myself. I called everyone to the hotel. Drew told me that they have found Jenna, but she is pretty beat up.

"What happened to you Jenna? I asked in a concerned tone. She didn't answer the question and told us to move on with the meeting. I explained to them that we are probably going into war, with what I don't know. I told them all about my experiences since the beginning, mike was new to all of this, and he was holding back his tears but will go to the death if he needed to. As I was telling them about what could be the end of our journey, I was holding back tears. They each came up to me and huddled around for a hug, we all said our goodbyes in advanced.

We all went our separate ways for the day and would meet back up later, mike and I would stay at the hotel for the night. "You scared mike? I understand if you're, because I'm scared too. The times are coming and we have to hit it head on." I said calmly. We stood there quietly for a good five minutes; he just stared out into space. I was going to try to say something to him but he walked outside and shut the door. Then my hands started to shake, the lights got really bright and I collapsed to the floor like I lost all feeling in my legs. I must have blacked out again; I was again in the hospital bed with friends and family standing around. Why am I having this vision again, could it mean something I wondered? I walked closer to the bed I was in and my face was cut up and my arms and legs had casts on them. I could never get this close before and I don't know what this means. Something is telling me this is really happening. The time and date on the clock read November 14th, 2025. I never really paid attention to the time and date before, maybe this is events to come and I'm seeing that we either won the battle or we lost and got lucky to still be alive. I looked around the room and a couple people were missing, mike and drew weren't in the room with me did they not make it, did they just leave the room. As I went to touch my body lying on the bed I felt a jolt of electricity hit my body and I woke up back in the hotel. I was trying to catch my breath as mike was standing over me; he just stared at me like I had died. "John, you ok? I thought you died or something" he said with a scared tone to his voice. I told him I was fine and that it happens all the time and not to be worried. I was just glad he was there to bring me back.

Chapter 8

It's been 4 days since my last blackout, I've been feeling weak and I know I might be dying. I need to pull myself together and get ready for war. "Mike, here take this, its sunglasses. I don't know what they will do for you besides block the sunlight from your eyes" I explained. I also told him we need to study these logs I received from this kid in Oklahoma City. We spent the next few hours watching the videos and reading the logs and we can't come up with anything. "This was such a big waste of time, john" mike yelled. I could see he was getting frustrated with all of the information he was given in a short amount of time. "Mike, are you ok to go along with this? I will understand if you want to back out" I explained. He told me that he just found me and that the thought of one of dying is hard to handle, but he will stick by my side. Drew and Sammy and Jenna came back and was ready to get down to business, they all looked rested and afraid at the same time. "John when is this happening, do you even know?" drew asked. I told him I don't know and all I did know is that it was coming and I was warned to stop. I then felt dizzy and light headed, could it be another blackout coming on, or worse? Soon visions started flashing in my mind like if I was looking at a bunch of pictures at once. I saw a building that looked like a school, and people everywhere. Like a reunion or a gathering, what could it mean?

"Oh my head, I had a vision of a school and there were people inside. Is there a reunion coming up soon?" I asked frantically. Sammy explained that a 10 year school reunion was scheduled this month. I told them we need to find more clues about what happened to my mother and at all costs, we can't back down and do whatever it takes.

Mike and I went to the library to try to find some ideas of where our mom went so we have to assume she died. "John, did you know her well?" he asked. I told him I didn't really know her that well. Since I can't remember anything from my childhood, my memories are gone and I need to get them back. "Mike, I don't know much about you, and I've only really known you for a few days." I said. "Well after high school, my father left us and it was just me and mom for a while and then she disappeared, then something about an accident. No survivors were found." He explained. I asked him what accident he was talking about, he said it was the one many years ago. I was getting shocked because I had a vision about me being in the hospital after an accident. "I wonder how much of this he does know." I thought to myself. I just stared at him for a moment, I was going to ask him a very serious question, but before I had a chance I blacked out again. But it didn't feel like the other blackouts, "what is going on" I thought to myself. It felt more like a dream, it was just dark no one around but me.

"Hello!" I yelled. The silence was killing me, maybe I was dead and I can finally relax. "I'm free" I thought to myself. A light appeared out of no where and was shining on a desk that wasn't there before. The desk had a folder and nothing else; it was a little creepy if you ask me, as I was looking through the folder I noticed that it was files about mike. according to these he is dead, but it cant be true because he looks real, feels real, and unfortunately smells real. "No, this cant be true, someone wake me up please!!!" I yelled at the top of my lungs. I fell to my knees and curled up into a ball, staring blankly into nothing just letting out all my frustration. "Mike, what happened?" I heard Sammy yelling. But he was no where to be seen, I looked around and started running toward his voice. "Sammy, I'm here!" I screamed. "Sammy, he just fell over I don't know what happened, it's like he blacked out again." he explained. "What do you mean again?" Sammy asked. Mike told him the story about earlier and Sammy seemed upset about it, all I could hear is Sammy and mike fighting. All of a sudden it got quite, no sound to be heard and I was getting worried.

All I could think about is them fighting and hoping they're both ok, why would they fight instead of trying to get help. I always wondered if it would be easier to end my life, so no one can get hurt. I've thought about it many times and it's tough to even think about, I just don't want this to go on any longer. "John, john you ok, come on open your eyes" mike said as I woke up from the hell I was in. "Why were you guys fighting? I asked. I told them that I was sick of this shit, I hate walking through life and that I wanted to end it all so no one would have to worry about me anymore. Out of the corner of my eye I saw Sammy turn around and plant a right hook to the side of my face. "What the hell was that for Sammy?" I asked holding my face. "You don't need to say that shit, john you're my friend and losing anyone is tough and to hear you say that hurts" he argued while holding back tears. A knock at the door stopped our argument; mike answered the door to find a police officer standing there. the officer asked some questions about a disturbance coming form the home, and mike as the smart ass he is told the cop we were having a lovers quarrel and shut the door on his face, me and Sammy just watched mike walk back laughing his ass off. "Well the bacon is gone, so where were we?" mike said laughing. We couldn't really talk or fight because we were laughing so hard.

Then jenny and drew came back with no news on where my mother is but they said that the school here in town wasn't always a school. It used to be an abandoned hospital for mentally ill patients, it closed down in the early 50's because there was a patient that had reoccurring blackouts and went completely crazy on all the staff. The patient latter died of an unknown cause. I asked them if the patient they were talking about had a name, and they stood silent and looked around at each other. Drew told me that it was my great grandfather, he totally lost it one day during a counseling session. They told me the article read that he had black eyes, and was ranting about some big apocalypse, and that "they" were coming. "They were coming?" I asked confused by the information I was given. The only thing I could think of is what is going to happen to me?

Chapter 9

It's been 2 weeks since my last vision; things are getting better between my friends and my brother. I also found out what those objects that were in the box were for, they're weapons to use against these flashers. I read more into what Jenna and Sammy found weeks ago, when the patient lost his mind to these flashers, apparently a great ancestor of mine took these objects and stopped the flashers in there tracts but something went wrong. By stopping the event my great ancestor died and one of the artifacts released the being. With the knowledge I have now, makes me wonder if these stupid objects will work against it. I recently tried going to a doctor to have them study my brain patterns and the test results showed no obstructions or anything else alarming. The doctor also told me I was in no danger and to ignore them, I told him everything from the first day to now and he told me I shouldn't be worried and that I would be fine. For almost a year now I'm not fine, I am fucking terrified of the events to come and the flashers that told me I'm in danger. I also had a dream the other night, I was on the ground and it was dark, mike, and Jenna were there looking down at me and I couldn't move. I saw a flickering light of some kind but couldn't make it out. Some smoke all around we and I could hear screaming, but I was paralyzed and couldn't move. Then I heard my name being called and I woke up, sweat was falling down my face like I was in a sauna for 2 hours. "Hey how is it going, how do you feel today?" drew asked while drinking a bud light he found in the fridge. "I'm feeling ok, I think. Really tired and worried" I told him. He told me I was going to be fine and we were going to stop this from happening. Then I heard a voice say "someone is going to die in 2 days time." I asked drew if he said something just now and he shook his head no. "You hearing things now?" he asked. I didn't say anything to him because I don't want them to be paranoid or feel like they are the ones that are going to die. "Where was the voice coming from? Are the blackouts and visions turning into telepathic signs now?" I asked myself. I keep wondering why this is happening to me and only 2 other people that I know of, the Youtube kid and this other kid in Oklahoma City. I thought maybe it could be an alien invasion and they are taking peoples memories for some secret plan of some kind. "Sammy, what are you doing?" I laughed as he was laying in some freakish way on the couch. "Nothing man just checking my social stream page." he muttered. I told everyone that we had to stop messing around and start focusing on the bigger picture at hand, we argued for hours how boring it is to figure out what the objects are and how to use them. I told them we need to use them to save ourselves from this evil, I looked around at them and they looked tired and worn out. "Everyone lets gets some rest we have a lot to do" I explained. We rested for days and it didn't seem to do much for us, we seemed weak and helpless. "So what are supposed to be doing?" drew asked frustrated with me. "We need to practice fighting" I said. "I think we have done a lot of that that last few days; I think we are masters at it now." Mike chimed in. he is always cracking wise to lighten the mood in the room, we all had a good laugh. Sammy and mike soon fell asleep and drew, Jenna and myself spent the rest of the time planning different scenarios that could take place. "I think this is coming along great guys" Jenna said in a soft tone. "We have only begun" I said. It was getting quite and cold, like the day in the police station. I looked around in fear, my eyes got wide and Jenna looked funny like she was frozen. A voice was speaking in my ear that I don't recognize, and then I sat there listening to the message

"Son, you need to be brave in the coming days, the battle will be challenging and fierce, trust in yourself and in your friends. I will be watching over you and good luck"

I then snapped out of the trance I was in, Jenna and drew just stared at me like I had something on my face. I told them that I think it's getting worse and those we might get over our heads on this one. A noise startled us as Sammy and mike jumped off the couches, we all looked around and didn't notice anything until mike found a paper on the ground. It looked like instructions to the objects we have, but when I found them this wasn't in there at all.

"What does it say?" I asked mike. He told us that there were a few instructions on how to use them, 1. Use the camera for a blinding light that will paralyze your enemy and keep them locked in place. 2. Sunglasses are used to see an invisible enemy and they make a cool accessory item. 3. The blank photo, never lose this EVER it is very important that you don't

The page cuts off there, we stared around at one another and we all looked confused. "So about this reunion, what the hell are we going to wear" mike asked. "Clothes dumb ass" Sammy snapped back. It seemed these two aren't getting along very well, and I don't know how that will help us in a battle. I told those to that they needed to kiss and make up and work out there differences or I will have to make them, I feel like a father to them and they are old enough to know how to be grown ups. "You know what you two, go to your rooms, you guys are grounded until I say other wise" I yelled. They both looked at me, and then looked at each other and rolled they're eyes and hugged it out. "Good I'm glad you ladies could make up" I laughed. I told them that in a few days we had the reunion and just act normal and try not to cause a scene or draw attention to ourselves, and mike that definitely goes for you. "Whatever man I'm awesome ill be fine" he laughed it off. "I suppose we should all get some sleep" Jenna muttered." I went to be scared and don't know how to feel or even know what to do. Only time will tell.

Chapter 10

As I was outside looking at the sky I could only feel the wind and the sunlight on my skin, it wasn't like any other day today. It felt like a day that could be our last day on earth, I had flash back of memories from my younger days. I remembered playing with my mom in the yard and all the friends I had in high school, the people I met in life and now it could all just be a distant memory now. "hey guys that paper was right I look freaking sexy with these sunglasses on" mike yelled." it was like 8am I don't know what he thinks by yelling that early, I didn't sleep well last night. I was to busy thinking about today and everyone around me; I'm going to kind of miss these guys. I still thinks its funny how after all this stuff has gone on I meet my brother and I think its to good to be true, after all I cant trust anyone and so far he seems legit. I could hear that Sammy and drew were awake because they like to race to the breakfast table every morning, so far drew has Sammy beat by 2 and Jenna thinks its stupid, but we just tell her it's a guy thing. "Morning everyone!" drew yelled as he dives into breakfast, I guess he could resist the smell of eggs and bacon in the morning.

Sammy doesn't like bacon much, but eats in anyway and mike eats everything that's not nailed down. If I didn't have to watch him he would eat everything on the table before everyone woke up. we talked for a good while and all washed up and changed for the big night tonight, mike is wearing jeans and a t-shirt, Jenna is wearing a red dress and a flower in her hair, drew and Sammy cant decide because they bought the same thing and don't want to look like twins, which they act like brothers anyway and me I'm keeping it simple, ill be a tux just because I look good in it. "You guys figure out what you are going to wear?" I asked drew and Sammy, since they were still arguing who was wearing what. I suggested that they just wear the same thing and to get over it and that they could just wear different ties.

Now that everyone is ready to go, we gathered up all our equipment and headed to the reunion. I haven't seen these people in forever and after this long I probably don't even know there names, even after looking at a year book so long ago. We will go and have a good time and home that the voices I heard are wrong, and that no one will get hurt or worse die tonight.

"I just wanted to let you guys know that I love all of you, and I'm glad to have you guys in my life. And if tonight goes the way I don't want it to, it was an honor fighting beside you guys." I said to them walking up to the school. They looked at me and each other and we had one big group hug, the older lady looked at us like we were freaks but we didn't care. "Tickets please?" the lady asked at the front door. Unfortunately only I drew and Jenna had a ticket, I told her that mike will be my plus one. She looked at me like an old person at a bus stop would look at you for cutting them off getting on the bus. Her face was wrinkly and she had really grey hair, not just hey you have a grey hair grey but the kind that if you were in the sun she would look bald. Her outfit was some 50's prom dress that shouldn't ever be worn again, and she smelled funny as well, like she hasn't taken a bath in a week. So we get into the gymnasium and it was packed with people, some were in suits and some were dressed casual.

The woman were all in dresses with there hair done up like they were going back to the prom. "Damn, there is some potential in here guys and gals" mike muttered softly. We all had a good laugh and mike was gone, on the dance floor apparently. "We have to put a bell on that kid, or we would never find him again" drew said. They had some old hip hop playing then it switched a slow country song "you want to dance with me?" Jenna asked with a school girl look on her face. I nodded my head and she whipped me onto the dance floor, she told me that she loved me and that she had a bad feeling about tonight as well. I told her everything was going to be ok and not to worry because I would protect her. The night so far was going smoothly with no signs of trouble, but I spoke to soon. The ground underneath us was shaking and lights were flickering. People were scrambling around and screaming, while we just stood there waiting to see who or what was coming.

It seemed like I was frozen and I couldn't move, I could see everyone around me and this wasn't a dream or it would be dark and cold. I felt a tingling and stinging pain like something was cutting me open, 5 black shadows blasted out of my chest and it felt like fire. I was still paralyzed and couldn't move to help anyone; they appeared to us as the old man, the older woman the young woman and the 2 kids. They wasted no time, and started attacking the helpless people in the gym, it was a hard site to see, all the blood and the bones being crushed and they hit the walls and the ground. I could hear mike yelling and I saw him run past me with a chair and when he got up to the old man he went right through him and I cant believe what happened next, the old man picked mike up by the throat and started levitating into the air and looked at me, and smiled and ripped him in half. I was screaming inside and I felt helpless, I let my brother die.

I finally was able to move, but I dropped to my knees and cried and screamed and then Jenna drew and Sammy picked me up and we ran outside in the rain. "Mikes gone, I let him die!" I cried out. We were behind the school and drew managed to grab mikes sunglasses before we got outside; we had to get them one at a time. drew guided us with finding them in the dark, "over there on your right, get the kids!" he yelled, as we ran up to a safe distance and Jenna took a picture of them with the camera and just as the instructions stated they froze in there tracts. But then a bright beam blasted out of the camera and the 2 kids were gone, they vanished into thin air. "It worked, it worked, and let's get the sons of bitches" Sammy yelled as he ran after the younger lady. but that too was short lived as she grabbed him by head and with 2 twits she popped it right off, his knees hit the ground first then he kind of just sat on his legs and didn't fall over. I can't believe what I'm seeing, we had no chance in hell of winning, I thought about giving up and just letting they take me. The rain was falling, thunder was cracking, and water was just dripping off my face as I looked around at all the dead bodies. I looked around and found Jenna and she had just taken another picture this time is of the older lady and again a bright beam blasted from the camera.

She looked at me with pride and then the pride went straight to fear and she looked down at her stomach and noticed she was bleeding from a sharp object was sticking out. "Noooo Jenna!" I yelled running toward her and just before I could get to her the younger lady who I thought was supposed to help me and the older man stopped me.

"We told you to stop, you didn't listen to us and now you pay the price." the younger lady yelled. I dropped to my knees with rain still dripping from my face, and blood every where. "I tried to prevent this from happening, I just wanted to find my mother and get my memory back!" I cried. Then a flash of light appeared behind the old man and the young lady, I thought it was the camera going off. But it wasn't and all I could hear was that female voice again "son, I'm here for you. Do you still have that blank photo?" she asked. The rain was frozen and so were the old man and the young lady. "You can use that photo to save one of your friends, only one so choose wisely, but I warn you son it will be at a cost." she said as she vanished and the rain came pounding down again. I sat there for a moment thinking about what that voice said, and I opened my eyes wide and smiled.

"I'm going beat you guys, I will not stand here and lose to you assholes!" I yelled as I ran toward them, I slid underneath them and grabbed the camera from Jenna's motionless body, and ran back into the gym. It was a long shot but I'm going to save my brother, I ran up to his body and held the blank photo in front of him and this big bright light rained down on him like something out of a movie. His body reconnected and snapped back into place and healed him, and then the young lady appeared behind him and told me she wouldn't allow this to happen. "Give up I have one, I don't need my memories anymore, I have the greatest one of them all and he is lying on the ground. I may have known him a short time but he gave up his life just like my friends to help me save the world and to help me as well" I explained with a big grin on my face. I then took a picture of her and with a beam of light I got rid of her. And with one to go mike got up from the ground and asked what happened and I explained to him that him and everyone had died. And that I would choose to save him for being the best younger brother ever, I told him it came at a cost and I told him to use the camera to save everyone else. "I love you bro, maybe one day we will meet again" I cried. Just before I left this world I heard my brother tell me he loved me too. Then a bright light came and I was somewhere wonderful, looked like... I was home. My mother was there and my father sitting at the table in the dinning room. I got my memories back without losing the last of them before I died, I stood there for a moment just to take in this happy moment and if I were to move forward and sit down with them it would me I'm really gone and there is no going back and smiled and took those few steps to the table "hi mom, hi dad."